A catalogue record for this book is available from the British Library

Published by Ladybird Books Ltd
A subsidiary of the Penguin Group
A Pearson Company
LADYBIRD and the device of a Ladybird are trademarks of Ladybird Books Ltd Loughborough Leicestershire UK

Disney's

TOY STORY

Ladybird

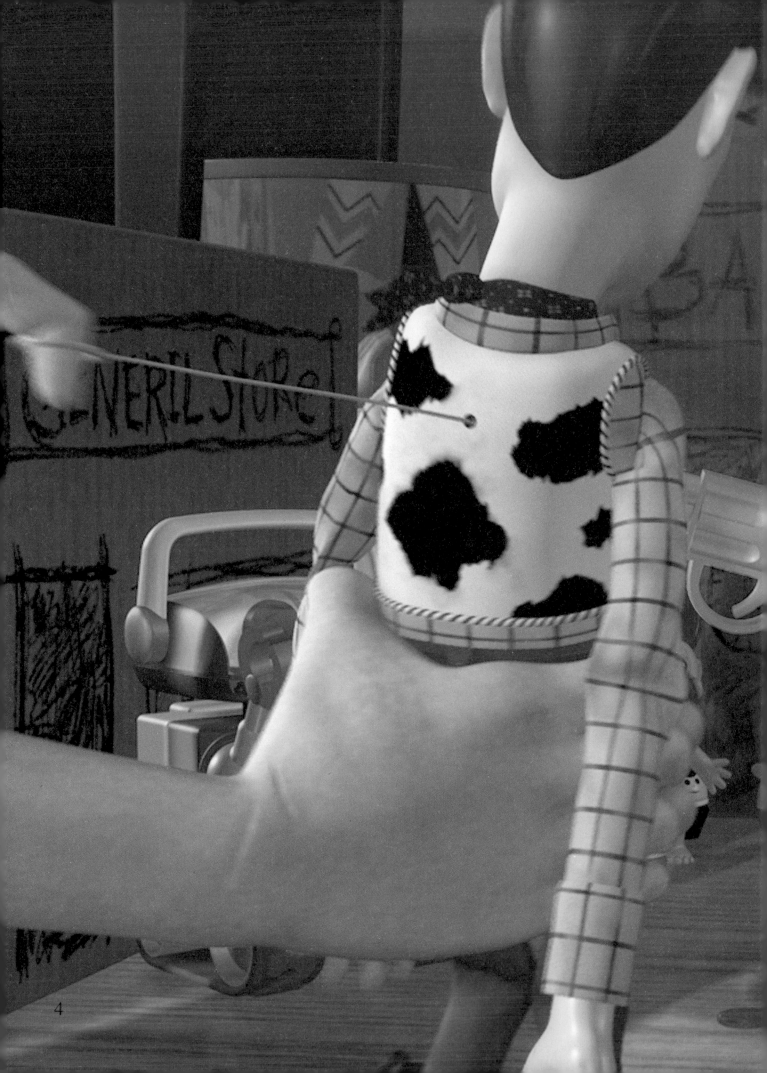

Woody the cowboy was Andy's favourite toy. Andy would make Mr Potato Head, Slinky Dog, Rex the dinosaur and Hamm the pig into bank robbers and Woody would always be there to save the day, and Bo Peep, the sweet shepherdess! "Reach for the sky!" the toy cowboy would say when Andy pulled the string on Woody's back.

But there was one thing Andy didn't know about his toys – when he left his bedroom, they came alive!

Today it was Andy's birthday party. He rushed downstairs to see the decorations his mum had chosen.

"This looks great!" Andy said to her. The room was hung with lots of balloons and streamers. Soon, his friends began to arrive for the party.

While Andy and his friends were playing downstairs, Woody and the other toys were upstairs in Andy's bedroom. Once Woody had made sure that Andy wasn't coming back for a while, he came to life! From the top of the bed he called out, "OK everybody, the coast is clear."

9

At Woody's call, the rest of Andy's toys began to stir as well. Woody asked Slinky Dog to gather everyone for a meeting, and soon Hamm, Rex, Bo Peep, Mr Potato Head and all the other toys were standing together, waiting to see what Woody had to say.

Woody soon called the meeting to order. Andy's family were moving house the following week and he wanted to make sure the toys were ready. "To make sure no toys are left behind I want everybody to get themselves a moving buddy. If you don't have one – get one!" he ordered. Then, trying to seem calm, Woody continued, "Oh, yes! Andy's birthday party has been moved – to today."

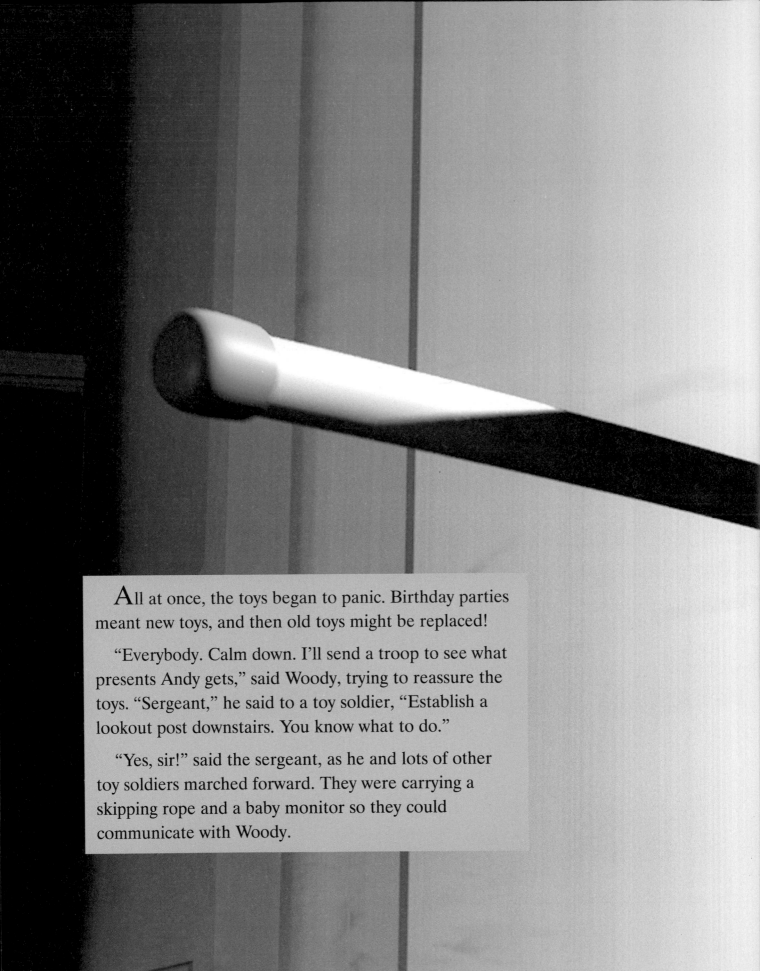

All at once, the toys began to panic. Birthday parties meant new toys, and then old toys might be replaced!

"Everybody. Calm down. I'll send a troop to see what presents Andy gets," said Woody, trying to reassure the toys. "Sergeant," he said to a toy soldier, "Establish a lookout post downstairs. You know what to do."

"Yes, sir!" said the sergeant, as he and lots of other toy soldiers marched forward. They were carrying a skipping rope and a baby monitor so they could communicate with Woody.

Once the soldiers had checked the coast was clear, some of them slid down the skipping rope while others parachuted into the observation area – a good viewing position to watch Andy as he opened his presents. The sergeant looked through his binoculars and began speaking into the baby monitor, "Andy's opening the first present…"

"It's a – lunch box," said the sergeant. The toys sighed with relief. For a while Andy didn't receive any toys and everyone relaxed. But suddenly the sergeant said, "Andy's mum has pulled out another present. Andy's opening it…"

Then the sergeant was cut off, and a moment later Andy and his friends burst into the bedroom! The toys froze…

19

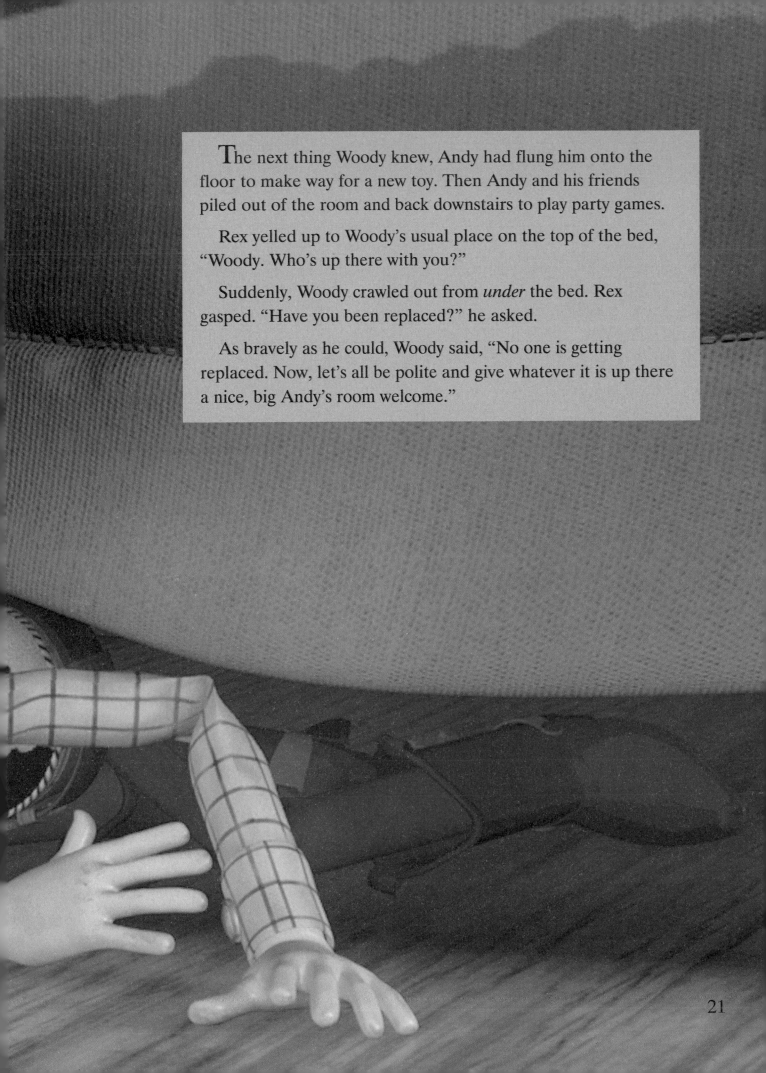

The next thing Woody knew, Andy had flung him onto the floor to make way for a new toy. Then Andy and his friends piled out of the room and back downstairs to play party games.

Rex yelled up to Woody's usual place on the top of the bed, "Woody. Who's up there with you?"

Suddenly, Woody crawled out from *under* the bed. Rex gasped. "Have you been replaced?" he asked.

As bravely as he could, Woody said, "No one is getting replaced. Now, let's all be polite and give whatever it is up there a nice, big Andy's room welcome."

Woody climbed up the side of the bed and peeked over the edge. He gulped nervously as he saw a large figure outlined against the bright window...

There, standing before him, was – Buzz Lightyear, Space Ranger.

Buzz didn't even notice Woody climb up onto the bed, he was too busy talking into the receiver on his wrist band. "Star Command," he was saying. "Do you read me?"

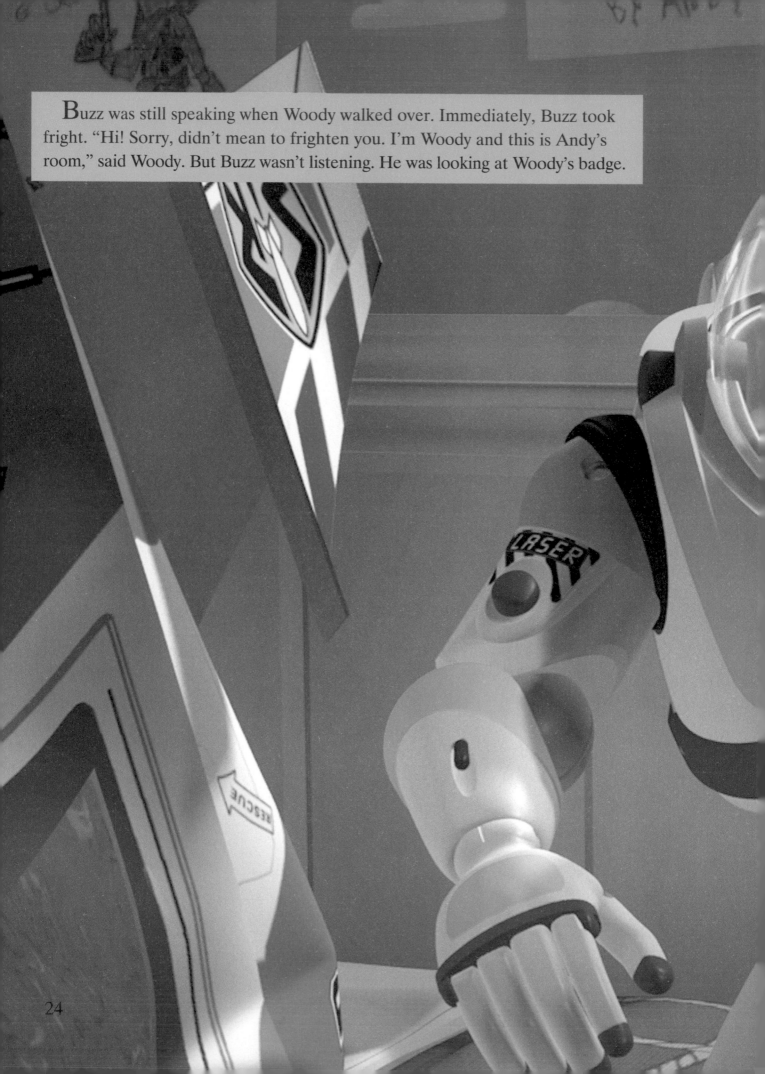

Buzz was still speaking when Woody walked over. Immediately, Buzz took fright. "Hi! Sorry, didn't mean to frighten you. I'm Woody and this is Andy's room," said Woody. But Buzz wasn't listening. He was looking at Woody's badge.

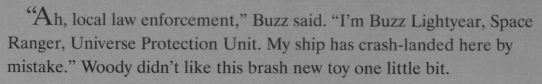

"Ah, local law enforcement," Buzz said. "I'm Buzz Lightyear, Space Ranger, Universe Protection Unit. My ship has crash-landed here by mistake." Woody didn't like this brash new toy one little bit.

The other toys climbed up to meet Buzz. Unlike Woody, they were all very impressed with the different gadgets that Buzz had.

Poor Woody soon found he had to defend his place as Andy's favourite toy, and as such, the leader of the toys. Trying to convince the others, he said, "Look, we're all very impressed with Andy's new toy, but…"

"Toy!" said Buzz. He couldn't believe his ears. He wasn't a toy, he was a real Space Ranger.

"Yes, that's right," replied Woody. "T-O-Y. Toy."

"I think the term you're searching for is 'Space Ranger'," said Buzz, calmly.

"You're not a Space Ranger. You're a toy," replied Woody.

"I am a Space Ranger," said Buzz.

"Okay then," said Woody, who was now getting rather annoyed, "prove it."

So yelling, "To infinity and beyond," Buzz leapt off the bed – he bounced onto a mobile and glided around the room a few times before making a perfect landing. Andy's toys were thrilled – except for Woody.

OPERATION

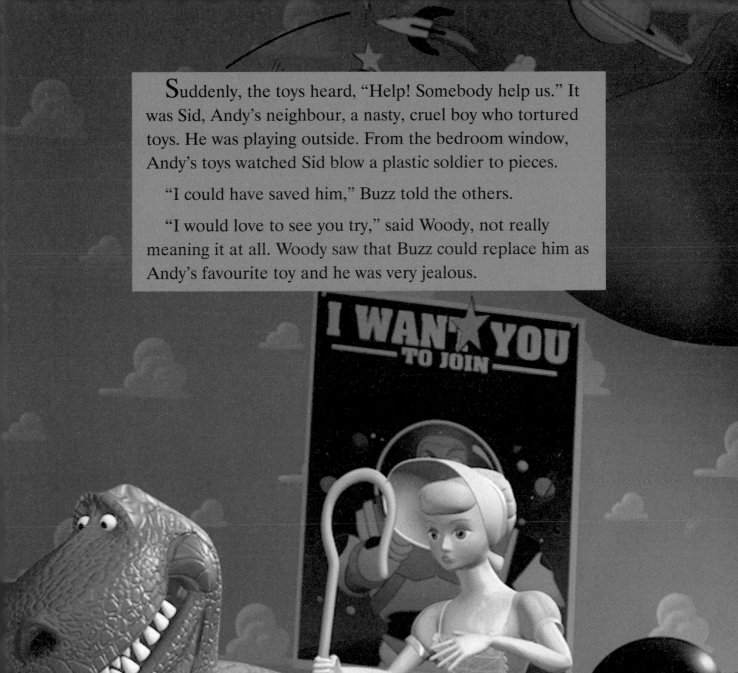

Suddenly, the toys heard, "Help! Somebody help us." It was Sid, Andy's neighbour, a nasty, cruel boy who tortured toys. He was playing outside. From the bedroom window, Andy's toys watched Sid blow a plastic soldier to pieces.

"I could have saved him," Buzz told the others.

"I would love to see you try," said Woody, not really meaning it at all. Woody saw that Buzz could replace him as Andy's favourite toy and he was very jealous.

Later that day, Andy and his mum were going to Pizza Planet for dinner. Andy was only allowed to take one toy with him and Woody wanted to be that toy. He sent the remote control car towards Buzz, hoping to knock him behind the desk. But everything went wrong and Buzz ended up falling out of the open window.

"Buzz!" cried all the toys, peering down into the garden to see if he was alright.

When there was no sight or sound of Buzz, the toys all looked accusingly at Woody.

"It was an *accident*," Woody pleaded.

"Let's string him up by his pull-string!" cried Mr Potato Head. Suddenly, Andy burst into the bedroom looking for Buzz. When he couldn't find him, he grabbed Woody instead. For the time being, Woody was safe.

33

But Buzz wasn't far away. He had fallen safely onto a bush below the window. As the family car pulled away from the house, Buzz grabbed onto the bumper. He wasn't going to let the cowboy get away with this.

When the car stopped at a petrol station and Andy and his mum got out, Buzz jumped in. He glared at Woody. "I want you to know that even though you tried to terminate me, revenge is not an idea we promote on my planet," he said.

"Oh, that's good," sighed Woody, grinning at Buzz. He thought he had been forgiven.

"But we're not on my planet, are we?" said Buzz, and charged at the cowboy. The two toys rolled over again and again until suddenly, they fell out of the car. That was when Andy and his mum drove away, leaving Buzz and Woody stranded.

Immediately, Buzz tried contacting Star Command for help. Woody went mad. "You are a toy!" he shouted. "An action figure. You are *not* real!"

But Buzz wouldn't believe him. Luckily, the two managed to hitch a lift to Pizza Planet on a delivery truck. Once inside, Buzz spotted a rocket-shaped crane game filled with little green alien toys. He was certain it was a spaceship to take him home and jumped in. Knowing he could never return to Andy's bedroom alone, Woody jumped in after him.

"I am Buzz Lightyear," Buzz told the aliens. "Who's in charge?"

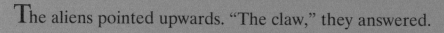

The aliens pointed upwards. "The claw," they answered.

Then someone shouted, "Hey, Bozo!" It was Sid. Mean, scary Sid. "A Buzz Lightyear!" he cried, and began lowering the crane.

As the crane grabbed Buzz and began lifting him upwards, Woody grabbed Buzz's legs and tried pulling him back down. But the crane was too strong and Sid soon had the two toys in his grasp. "Alright!" he yelled, seeing both Buzz and Woody. "Double prizes!"

Back at Sid's house, Woody and Buzz were terrified. Sid broke up his toys and made them into weird-looking mutants!

Luckily, Buzz and Woody were saved from immediate danger when Sid was called downstairs for tea. Seizing their chance, Buzz and Woody slipped out of Sid's room.

Suddenly, Buzz covered Woody's mouth with his hand. "Be quiet," he whispered. Right in front of them was Scud, Sid's nasty dog, asleep in the hall. "Time to split up!" said Buzz.

Woody ran into a cupboard. Buzz was about to do the same when he thought he heard Star Command calling him. Delighted, he made his way towards the sound. "Calling Buzz Lightyear. Come in, Buzz Lightyear. This is Star Command," said a voice from a television in an upstairs room.

Buzz was overjoyed until he also heard the voice say, "Buzz Lightyear. The world's greatest toy!" So, Woody had been right after all – he *wasn't* real, he was just an ordinary toy. In one last effort to prove them all wrong, he climbed to the top of the stairs and tried to fly. But Buzz couldn't really fly and he crashed to the floor, breaking his arm off. As Buzz lay on the floor, Hannah, Sid's sister, found him and took him to her bedroom. She dressed Buzz up and made him join the tea party she was having with her dolls.

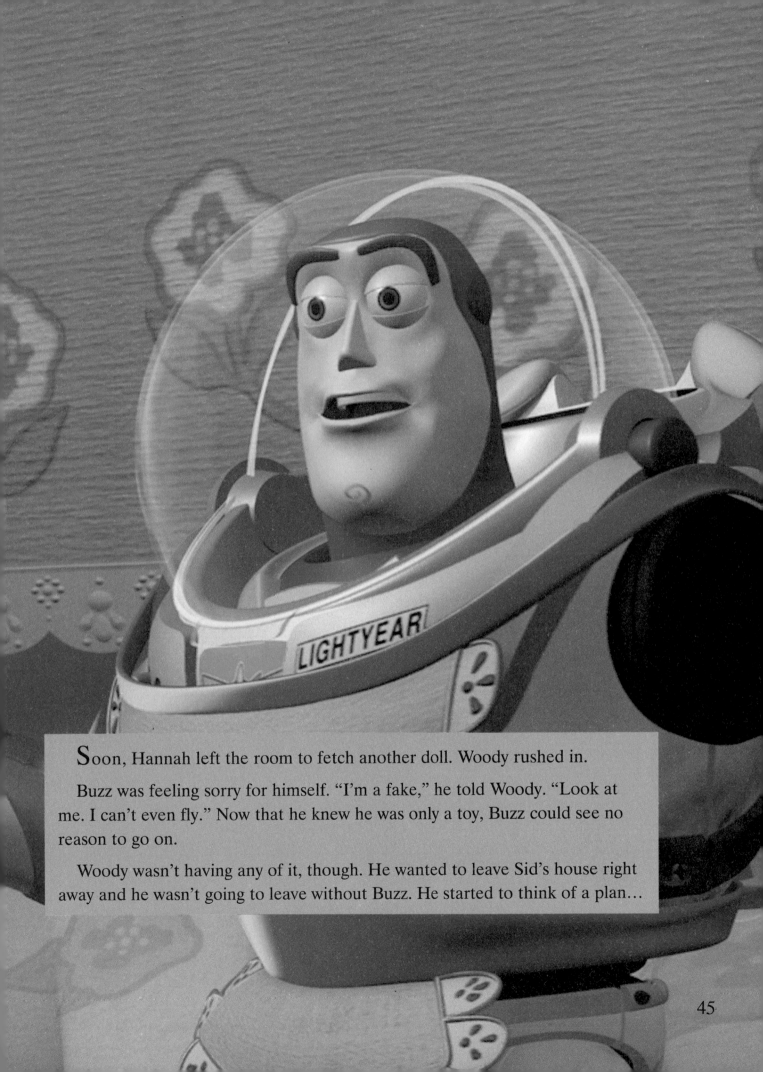

Soon, Hannah left the room to fetch another doll. Woody rushed in.

Buzz was feeling sorry for himself. "I'm a fake," he told Woody. "Look at me. I can't even fly." Now that he knew he was only a toy, Buzz could see no reason to go on.

Woody wasn't having any of it, though. He wanted to leave Sid's house right away and he wasn't going to leave without Buzz. He started to think of a plan…

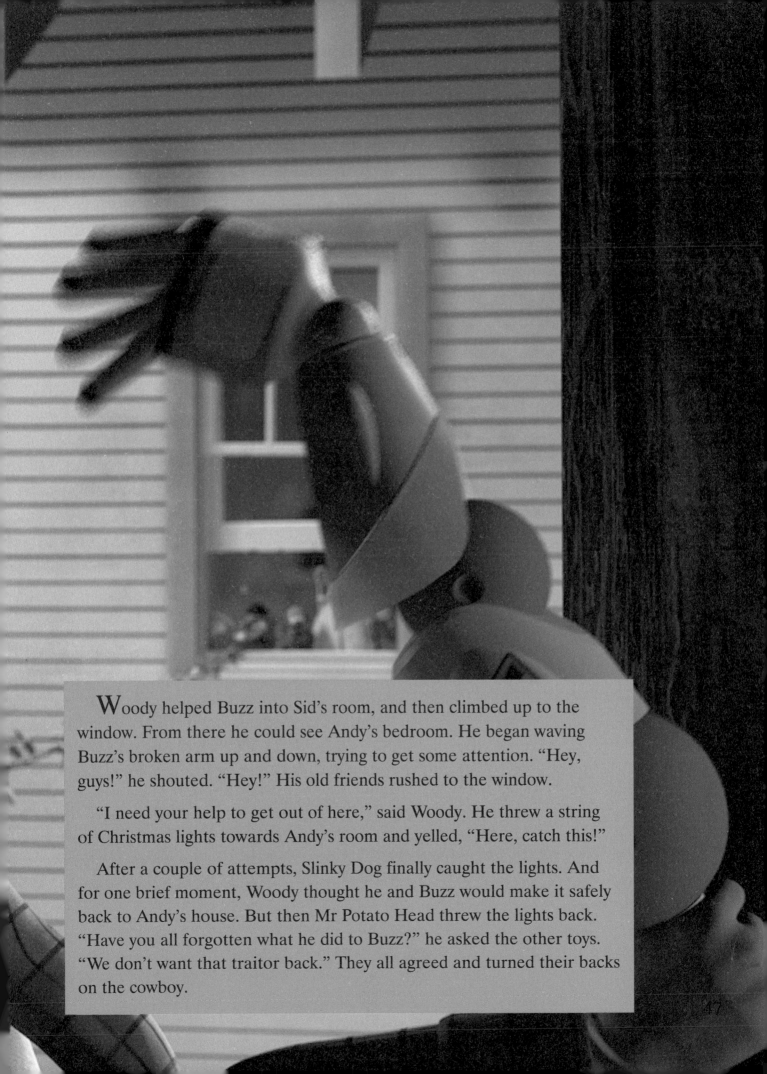

Woody helped Buzz into Sid's room, and then climbed up to the window. From there he could see Andy's bedroom. He began waving Buzz's broken arm up and down, trying to get some attention. "Hey, guys!" he shouted. "Hey!" His old friends rushed to the window.

"I need your help to get out of here," said Woody. He threw a string of Christmas lights towards Andy's room and yelled, "Here, catch this!"

After a couple of attempts, Slinky Dog finally caught the lights. And for one brief moment, Woody thought he and Buzz would make it safely back to Andy's house. But then Mr Potato Head threw the lights back. "Have you all forgotten what he did to Buzz?" he asked the other toys. "We don't want that traitor back." They all agreed and turned their backs on the cowboy.

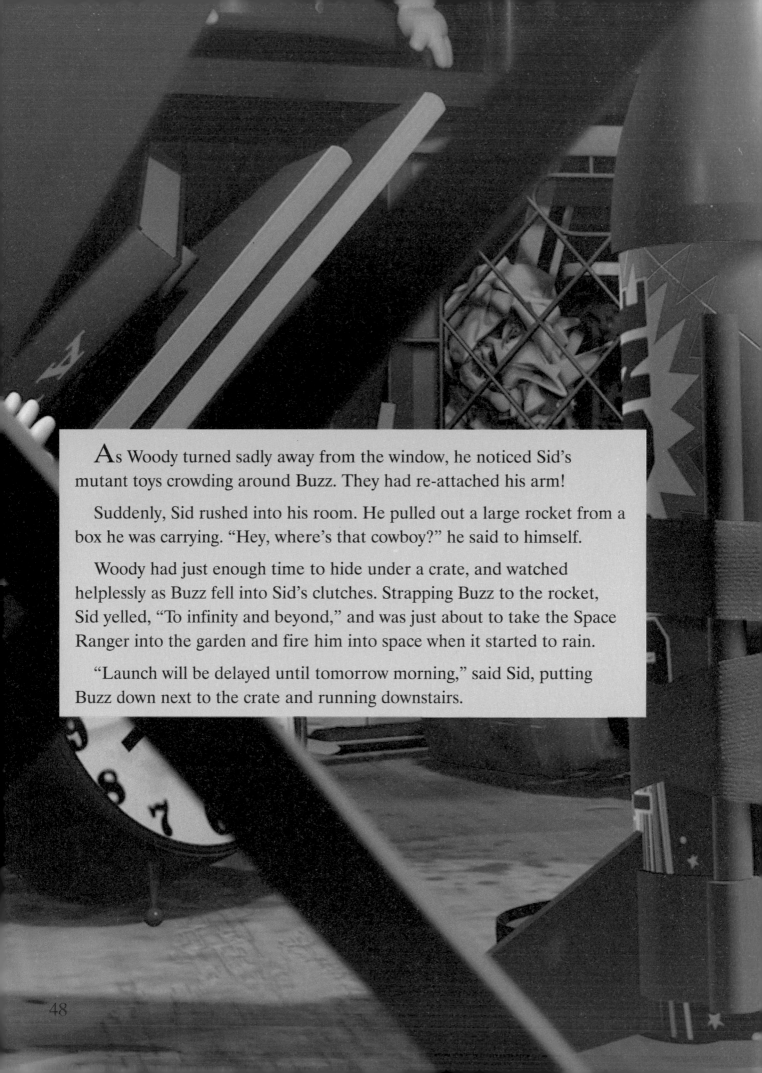

As Woody turned sadly away from the window, he noticed Sid's mutant toys crowding around Buzz. They had re-attached his arm!

Suddenly, Sid rushed into his room. He pulled out a large rocket from a box he was carrying. "Hey, where's that cowboy?" he said to himself.

Woody had just enough time to hide under a crate, and watched helplessly as Buzz fell into Sid's clutches. Strapping Buzz to the rocket, Sid yelled, "To infinity and beyond," and was just about to take the Space Ranger into the garden and fire him into space when it started to rain.

"Launch will be delayed until tomorrow morning," said Sid, putting Buzz down next to the crate and running downstairs.

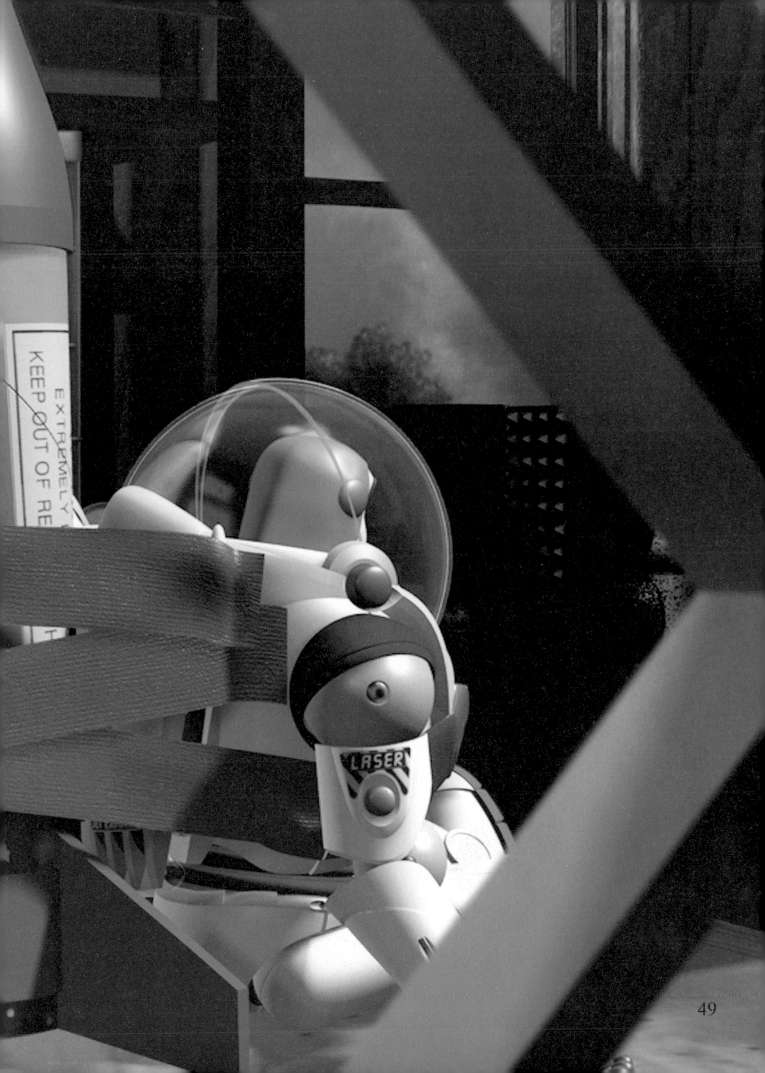

That night, as Sid slept, Woody pleaded for Buzz's help. He had become trapped beneath the crate. "Buzz, I can't get out without you. I need your help."

But Buzz was very depressed. "I can't help anyone. I'm useless," he sighed.

Woody felt sorry for Buzz. "Over in that house," said Woody, pointing towards Andy's bedroom, "is a kid who thinks you're the greatest. And it's not because you're a Space Ranger, it's because you're a toy. You're *his* toy." Woody's heartfelt words finally brought Buzz to his senses. At that moment, the toy cowboy realised that Buzz was his friend, too.

"Come on, Sheriff," said Buzz, standing on top of the crate trying to get Woody free. "There's a kid in that house who needs us. Now, let's get you out of this."

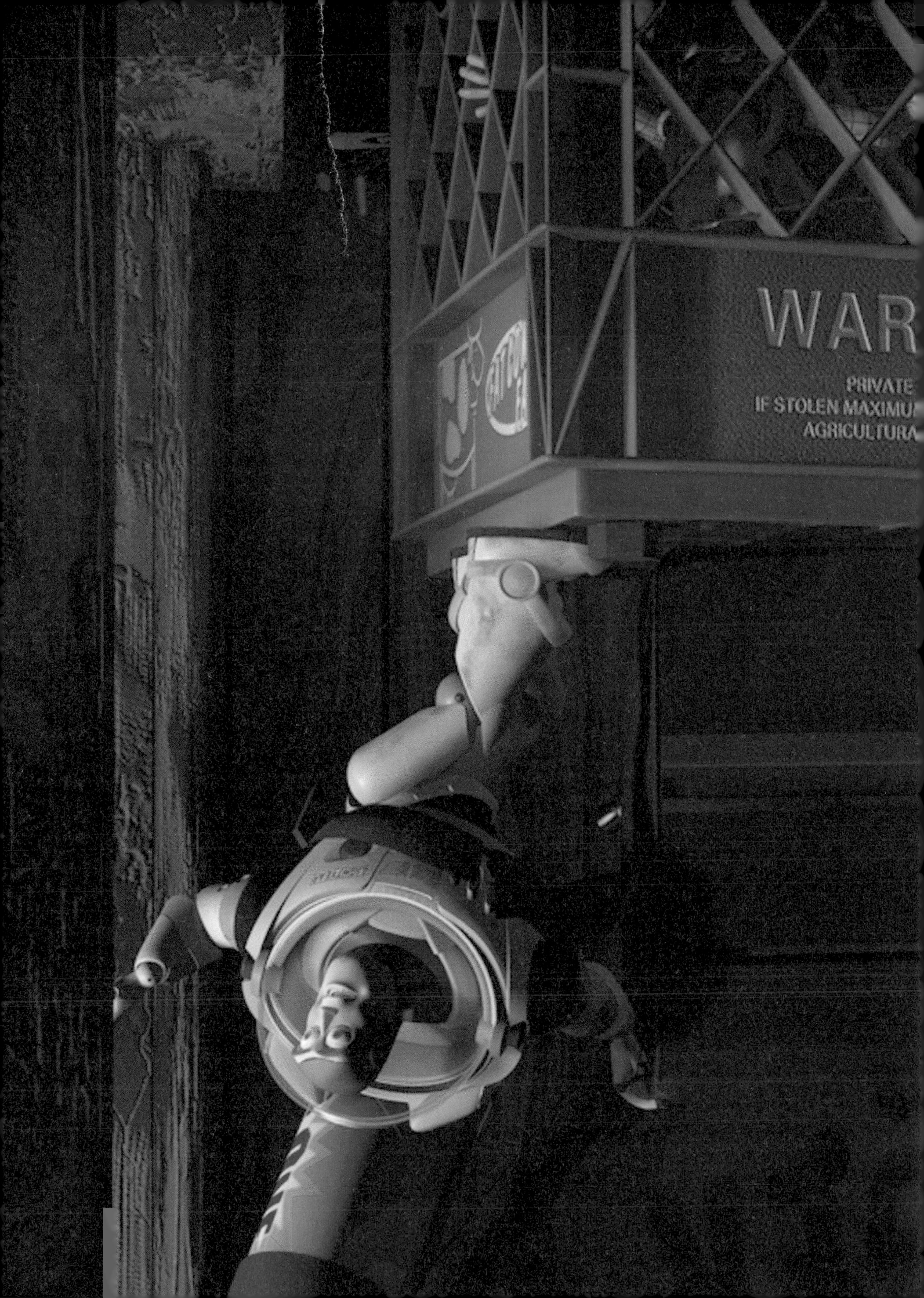
PRIVATE

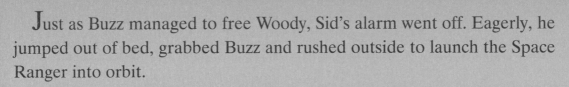

Just as Buzz managed to free Woody, Sid's alarm went off. Eagerly, he jumped out of bed, grabbed Buzz and rushed outside to launch the Space Ranger into orbit.

Woody was at a loss. How could he help his friend now? Then he remembered Sid's mutant toys. Coaxing them out from under the bed, he told them, "There's a good toy down there and he's going to be blown to bits in a few minutes. We've got to save him, but I need your help. I have a plan." And he quickly told the mutant toys his idea…

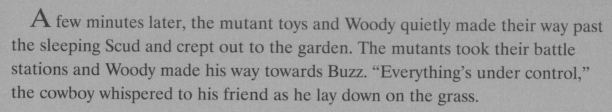

A few minutes later, the mutant toys and Woody quietly made their way past the sleeping Scud and crept out to the garden. The mutants took their battle stations and Woody made his way towards Buzz. "Everything's under control," the cowboy whispered to his friend as he lay down on the grass.

"Houston, all systems are go," said Sid, coming out of the shed with a box of matches. Then he saw Woody. "How'd you get out here?" he asked. He picked Woody up and threw him onto a grill. "You and I can have a barbecue later," sneered Sid and walked over towards Buzz.

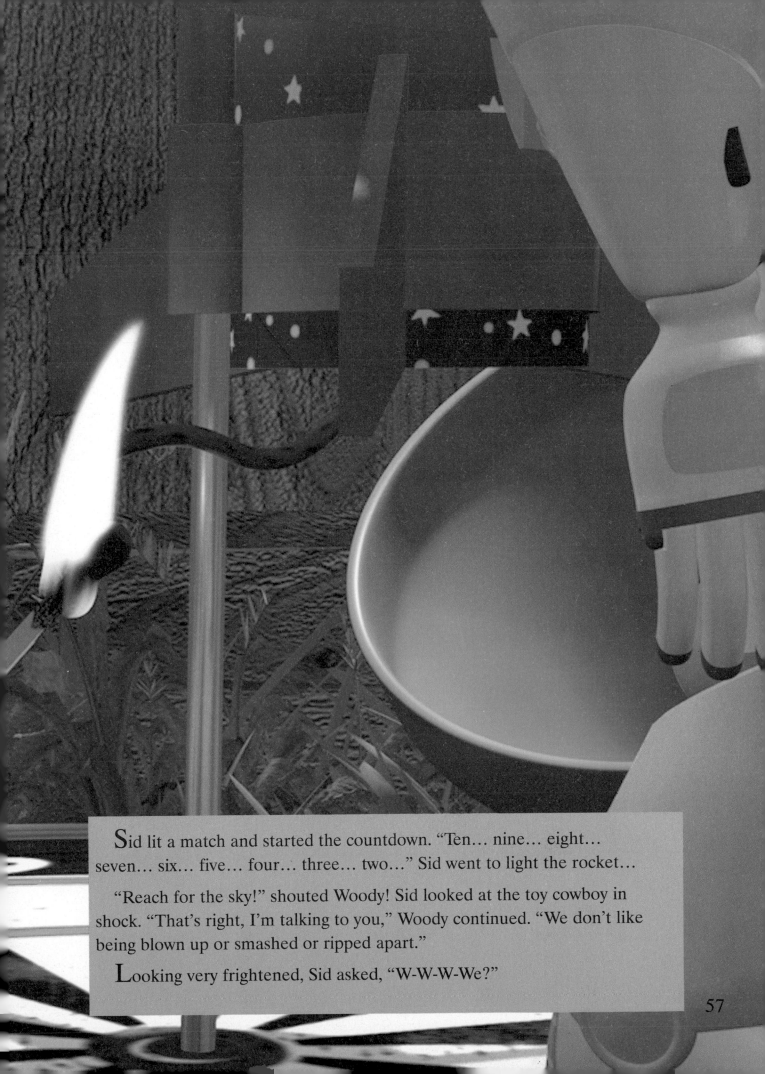

Sid lit a match and started the countdown. "Ten… nine… eight… seven… six… five… four… three… two…" Sid went to light the rocket…

"Reach for the sky!" shouted Woody! Sid looked at the toy cowboy in shock. "That's right, I'm talking to you," Woody continued. "We don't like being blown up or smashed or ripped apart."

Looking very frightened, Sid asked, "W-W-W-We?"

"That's right," said Woody. "Your toys." Sid's mutant toys rose up and started to close in on him slowly but surely. In terror, Sid ran back into his house.

Suddenly, they heard Andy's family saying goodbye to the house. If Woody and Buzz were going to get onto that removal van they had to go – now!

The two friends ran desperately towards the van. Buzz just managed to grab hold of a chain dangling from the back and hauled himself up. He turned around expecting to see Woody…

Woody had almost made it when Scud made a lunge for him. Now Woody was trapped between the van and the dog. Quickly jumping onto Scud's nose, Buzz managed to stop the dog in his tracks and Woody clambered onto the van. Now there was only one other problem – Woody was safe on the van but Buzz, who had jumped off Scud's nose, was back on the road!

Forcing his way into the van, Woody found a box labelled ANDY'S TOYS. He hurriedly opened it, grabbed the remote control car and pushed it out of the van to rescue Buzz.

But, still convinced that Woody was up to no good, the other toys attacked him. "Toss him overboard," ordered Mr Potato Head and they threw Woody over the edge of the van onto the road.

Luckily for Woody, Buzz whizzed by in the remote control car and picked him up before any more time was lost.

"Thanks," a relieved Woody said. "Now, let's catch up with that van."

Back on the van, Bo-Peep suddenly spotted Woody and Buzz drawing closer to them.

"Look!" she cried. "Woody was telling the truth." Feeling terrible for doubting Woody, the toys were determined to help, but it was too late. The car's batteries had run down. The toys watched Woody and Buzz disappear into the distance.

64

"Great," said Woody, not meaning it at all. But Buzz wasn't giving up yet. "Woody! The rocket!" he cried.

After a few false attempts, Woody managed to light the rocket's fuse. Suddenly, they shot off into the sky.

Closer and closer to the lorry the toys flew. Then Woody lost his grip on the remote control car. Luckily, the car floated safely into the removal van and Buzz and Woody flew higher and higher across the sky.

"Hey, Buzz! You're flying!" cried Woody, excitedly.

"Technically, I'm gliding," said Buzz. "But let's not spoil the moment."

And so the two friends hurtled through the sky with Woody yelling, "To infinity and beyond!" Then, he looked down to see something a little frightening, "Uh, Buzz," he said. "We've missed the van."

"We're not aiming for the van!" cried Buzz.

The Space Ranger suddenly made a graceful loop and headed straight for the open sun-roof of Andy's car. Then he executed a perfect dive, straight into a box on the seat next to Andy.

"Hey, wow!" cried Andy with glee, suddenly spotting the pair next to him. "Woody! Buzz! They've been in the car all the time," he said to his mum, and gave his two favourite toys a big hug.

A few months later, it was Christmas morning. Andy's family had settled happily in their new home and the toys were listening to the baby monitor once again.

"Frankincense, this is Myrrh. Come in," said the toy sergeant in code, from his command post downstairs.

All the toys were keen to find out what Andy's presents were. Everyone listened closely…

The sergeant spoke. "Andy's opening his present. I can't quite see…" Suddenly, lots of crackling cut the sergeant off.

"You're not worried, Buzz, are you?" teased Woody.

"Me? No, no," said Buzz. "Are you?"

Woody laughed. "What could Andy possibly get that would be worse than you?" he said. Then over the baby monitor came the answer — an excited barking.

Andy shrieked with delight. "Wow! A *puppy*!"